Zishe the STRONGMAN

This **PJ BOOK** belongs to

Madison aleeseawexller

pj Library®

JEWISH BEDTIME STORIES and SONGS

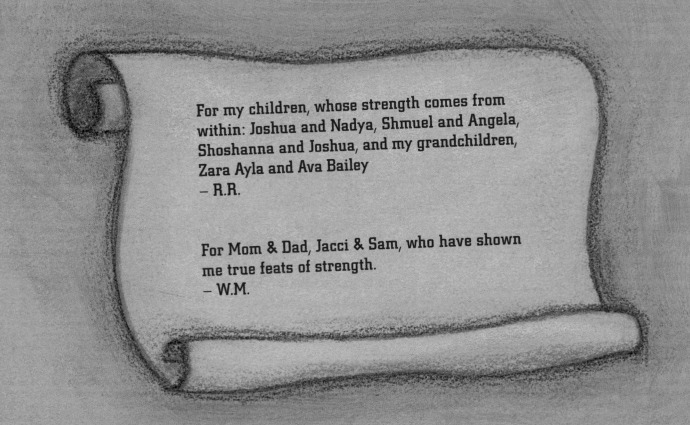

For my children, whose strength comes from within: Joshua and Nadya, Shmuel and Angela, Shoshanna and Joshua, and my grandchildren, Zara Ayla and Ava Bailey
– R.R.

For Mom & Dad, Jacci & Sam, who have shown me true feats of strength.
– W.M.

Zishe the Strongman is based on the life of **Siegmund Breitbart**, known as **"Zishe of Lodz"** (1883-1925)

Text copyright © 2010 by Robert Rubinstein
Illustrations copyright © 2010 by Lerner Publishing Group

The photograph on p. 32 appears courtesy of Bildarchiv Pisarek/akg-images.

Kar-Ben Publishing
A division of Lerner Publishing Group, Inc.
241 First Avenue North
Minneapolis, MN 55401 U.S.A.

Website address: www.karben.com

Library of Congress Cataloging-in-Publication Data

Rubinstein, Robert E.
    Zishe the strongman / by Robert Rubinstein ; illustrated by Woody Miller.
        p.   cm.
    ISBN 978-0-7613-3958-8 (lib. bdg. : alk. paper)
    1. Breitbart, Zishe, 1883-1925–Juvenile literature. 2. Strong men–United States–Biography–Juvenile literature. 3. Strong men–Poland–Biography–Juvenile literature. 4. Jews–United States–Biography–Juvenile literature. 5. Jews–Poland–Biography–Juvenile literature. 6. New York (N.Y.)–History–1898-1951–Juvenile literature. 7. Poland–Biography–Juvenile literature. I. Miller, Woody, ill. II. Title. III. Title: Zishe the strong man.
CT9997.B73R835 2010
974.7'1043092–dc22 [B]   2009001875

Manufactured in the United States of America
3 – CG – 10/25/13

011412.5K3

Zishe
the STRONGMAN

Robert RUBINSTEIN

illustrations by **Woody** MILLER

KAR-BEN
PUBLISHING

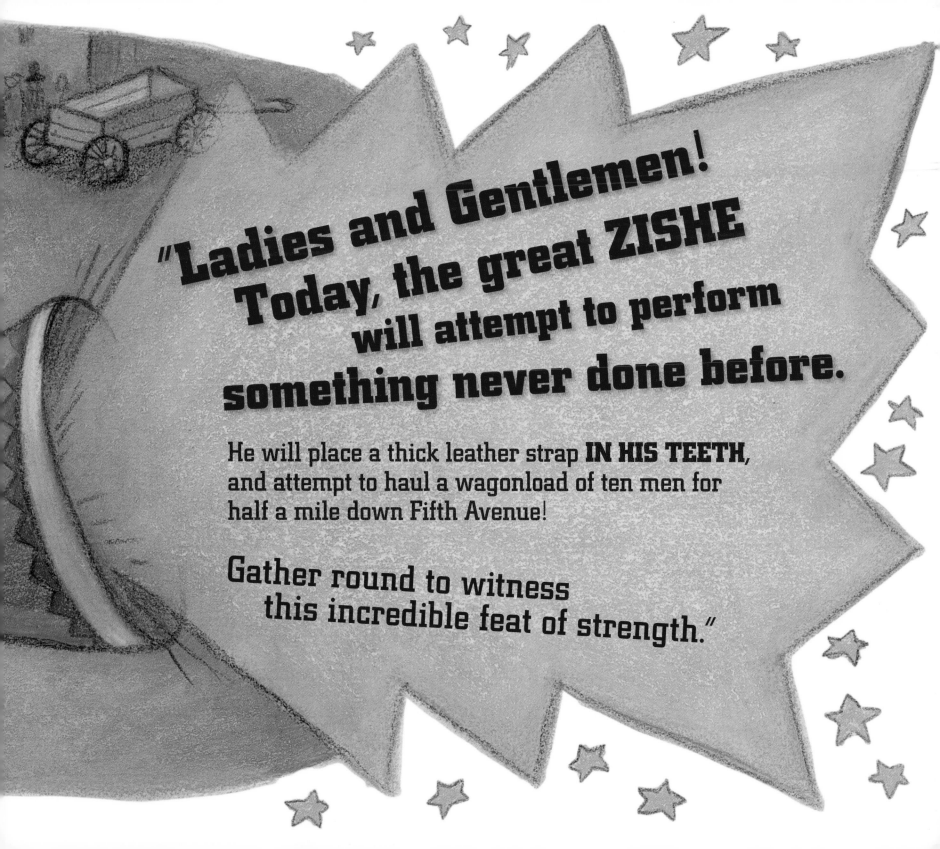

"**Ladies and Gentlemen! Today, the great ZISHE will attempt to perform something never done before.**

He will place a thick leather strap **IN HIS TEETH**, and attempt to haul a wagonload of ten men for half a mile down Fifth Avenue!

Gather round to witness this incredible feat of strength."

Who would have thought that a Polish Jew, son of a poor blacksmith, would become the strongest person in the world?

When Zishe was three years old, he loved to watch his father work. He would pick up a nine-pound hammer, swing it round, and pound it on the anvil. He laughed when he heard the crashing noise it made.

As Zishe grew older, the village children would bring him things to test his strength.

"Here, Zishe," they would say. "Can you bend this metal bar?" Zishe, just seven years old, would bend it easily.

"This is a thick chain, Zishe," they dared him. "I bet you can't snap it in half!" But that's exactly what Zishe did.

By the time Zishe turned eleven, there was not a bar that he could not bend or a chain that he could not snap.

But Zishe was also gentle. He loved small animals. He would hold tiny mice in his hands, and he loved to feed nuts to the squirrels.

Zishe also liked listening to music and learned to play the cello. To earn money for music lessons, he used his strength to haul and carry things for others.

As the years passed, Zishe's fame as a strongman spread throughout Poland. Strangers would come to town to challenge his strength.

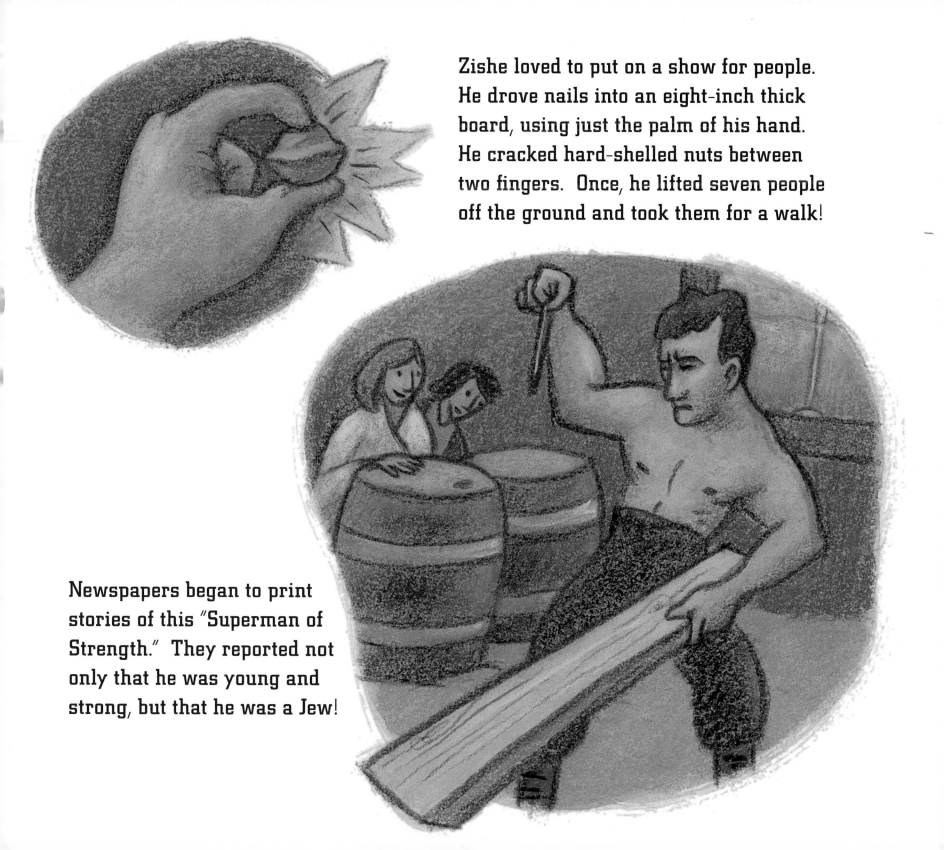

Zishe loved to put on a show for people. He drove nails into an eight-inch thick board, using just the palm of his hand. He cracked hard-shelled nuts between two fingers. Once, he lifted seven people off the ground and took them for a walk!

Newspapers began to print stories of this "Superman of Strength." They reported not only that he was young and strong, but that he was a Jew!

A stranger came to the blacksmith shop one day.

"I am Helmut Reiner from Vienna," he introduced himself. "I produce the most splendid shows. We travel to Paris, Rome, Venice, and even to London. I want you to perform great feats of strength for my audiences. You will become famous throughout Europe."

Zishe put down his horseshoe. He would be sad
to leave the village he loved, but he did not want
to be a blacksmith all his life. With his parents'
blessings, Zishe left his home to travel the world.

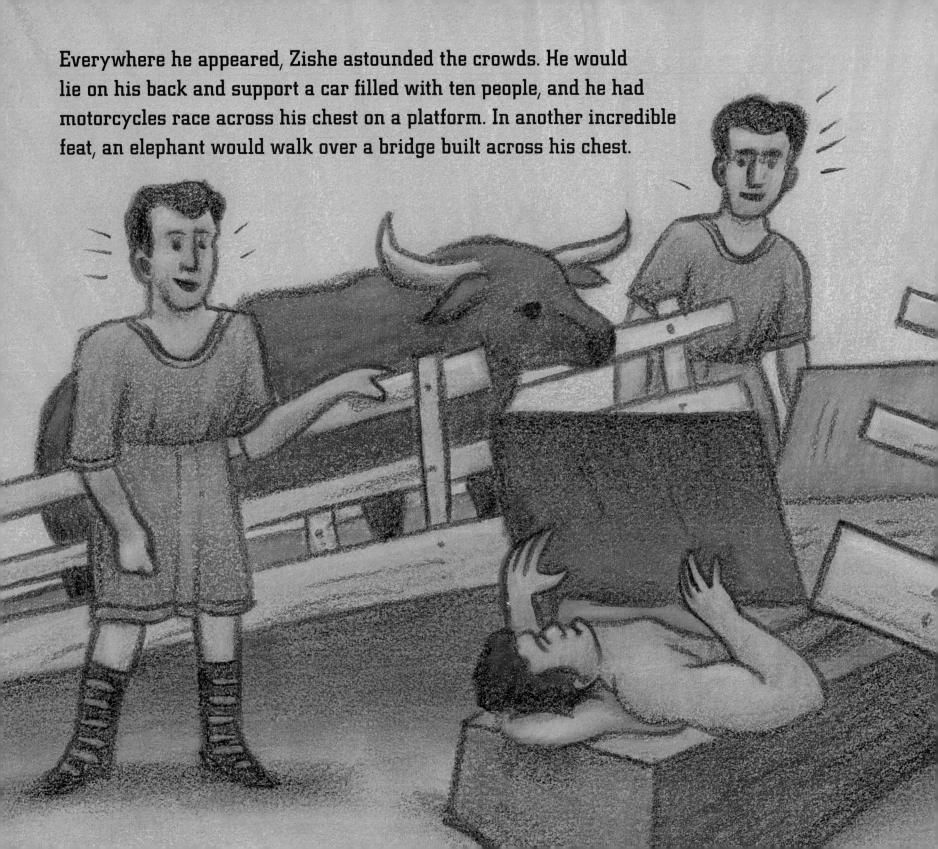

Everywhere he appeared, Zishe astounded the crowds. He would lie on his back and support a car filled with ten people, and he had motorcycles race across his chest on a platform. In another incredible feat, an elephant would walk over a bridge built across his chest.

Whenever he came to a town or city, Zishe would visit the Jewish community. He would lift children high into the air, and they would cheer him as their hero, a new Samson.

One day Zishe received an invitation from B.F. Keith's Vaudeville Shows to come and perform in America.

When the ocean liner docked in New York Harbor, a great crowd of actors, wrestlers, and other famous athletes were waiting to greet the "Superman of Strength."

When a reporter asked Zishe how he kept so strong and healthy, he replied, "I train hard, eat good foods, and I pray to God." Then he lifted his huge trunk, his cello case, and three heavy suitcases and walked through the streets to his hotel.

As he traveled throughout America, Zishe would take time to visit his fellow Jews. Often he would play his cello for children at local hospitals. His heart was as great as his strength.

"I would like your attention, please!
I need ten volunteers to sit in this wagon."

Then he selected ten of the
biggest men he could find.

"Now let me introduce the strongest man in the world—

the ONE AND ONLY **ZISHE**!"

The people cheered and applauded.

Zishe walked to the wagon. He removed his flaming red
cloak. He loosened and flexed his muscles and concentrated.

Zishe placed the leather strap between his teeth, biting down hard. He squatted, bracing his powerful legs. Suddenly, Zishe surged upwards and forwards. His muscles bulged and strained. Sweat poured down his face and chest. Nothing happened.

People held their breath. Maybe this was too much even for Zishe.

Zishe continued to strain forward—and then the wagon wheels started to turn—just a little—and then a little more— and more! The wagon with its load of ten men slowly rolled down Fifth Avenue. As it gained speed, the crowd went wild!

It was the crowning
achievement for
The Iron King!

ZISHE *LIVED!*

Zishe's real name was Siegmund Breitbart. He was born in 1883, the son of a blacksmith. He grew up with a love for music and poetry, and the ability to astonish others with his great power and strength.

When Zishe came to America, *The New York Times* (August 27, 1923) wrote: "The Polish strongman, who says that he is so sensitive that he would walk in a roadway to avoid treading upon a worm, arrived yesterday on the Hamburg-American liner *Albert Ballin*... He claims to be able to lift twelve persons in his hands, twist bars of iron like scraps of paper, crack Brazil nuts between his fingers and haul a wagon of ten people along the road with his teeth."

Zishe thought the Jewish people should be strong. In the 1920s he formed a Jewish sports group, hoping it would become an army to liberate the Jewish homeland (today the State of Israel). Unfortunately, he did not live to fulfill this dream.

After his incredible show on Fifth Avenue, Zishe continued to perform across America. Several months later he returned to Vienna. While performing one of his feats, a nail pierced his leg and he contracted blood poisoning. Despite a number of operations to stem the infection, he died eight weeks later at the age of 42.